William's Doll

William's Doll

by CHARLOTTE ZOLOTOW

pictures by WILLIAM PÈNE DU BOIS

HarperCollins*Publishers*

To Billy and Nancy

Text copyright © 1972 by Charlotte Zolotow
Pictures copyright © 1972 by William Pène du Bois
All rights reserved. Manufactured in China.
Library of Congress Cataloging Card Number: 70-183173
ISBN 0-06-027047-0
ISBN 0-06-443067-7
ISBN 0-06-027048-9 (lib. bdg.)

William wanted a doll.
He wanted to hug it
and cradle it in his arms

and give it a bottle

and take it to the park

and push it in the swing

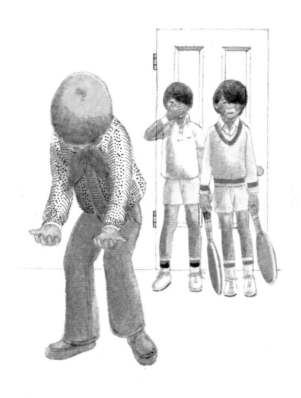

and bring it back home

and undress it

and put it to bed

and pull down the shades

and kiss it goodnight

and watch its eyes close

and then

William wanted to wake it up

in the morning

when the sun came in

and start all over again
just as though he were its father
and it were his child.

"A doll!" said his brother.

"Don't be a creep!"

"Sissy, sissy, sissy!" said the boy next door.

"How would you like a basketball?"
his father said.
But William wanted a doll.
It would have blue eyes
and curly eyelashes
and a long white dress
and a bonnet
and when the eyes closed
they would make a little click
like the doll that belonged
to Nancy next door.
"Creepy" said his brother.
"Sissy sissy" chanted the boy next door.

And his father brought home

a smooth round basketball

and climbed up a ladder

and attached a net to the garage

and showed William

how to jump as he threw the ball

so that it went

through the net

and bounced down

into his arms again.

He practiced a lot

and got good at it
but it had nothing to do

with the doll.

William still wanted one.

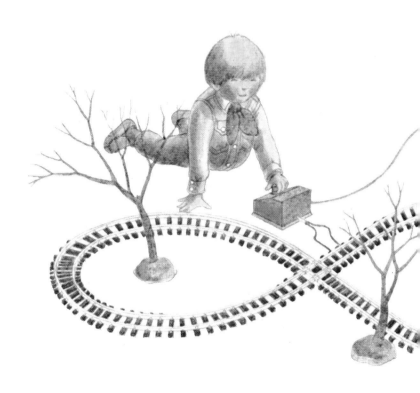

His father brought him an electric train.

They set it up on the floor

and made an eight out of the tracks

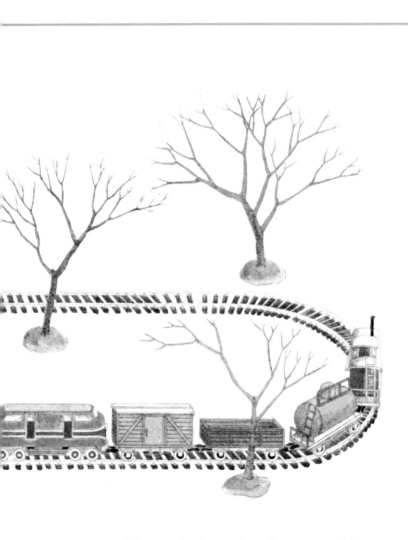

and brought in twigs from outside

and set them in clay

so they looked like trees.

The tiny train

threaded around and around the tracks

with a clacking sound.

William made cardboard stations

and tunnels
and bridges
and played with the train
a lot.

But he didn't stop wanting

a doll

to hug

and cradle

and take to the park.

One day

his grandmother came to visit.

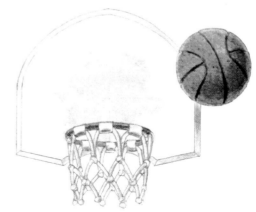

William showed her

how he could throw the ball

through the net

attached to the garage outside.

He showed her the electric train

clacking along the tracks

through the tunnel

over the bridge

around the curve

until it came to a stop

in front of the station

William had made.

She was very interested
and they went for a walk together
and William said,
"but you know
what I really want
is a doll."
"Wonderful," said his grandmother.
"No," William said.
"My brother says
it will make me a creep
and the boy next door
says I'm a sissy
and my father
brings me
other things
instead."
"Nonsense," said his grandmother.

She went to the store and

chose a baby doll

with curly eyelashes

and a long white dress

and a bonnet.

The doll had blue eyes

and when they closed

they made a clicking sound

and William loved it

right away.

But his father was upset.

"He's a boy!" he said

to William's grandmother.

"He has a basketball

and an electric train

and a workbench

to build things with.

Why does he need a doll?"

William's grandmother smiled.

"He needs it," she said,

"to hug

and to cradle

and to take to the park

so that

when he's a father

like you,

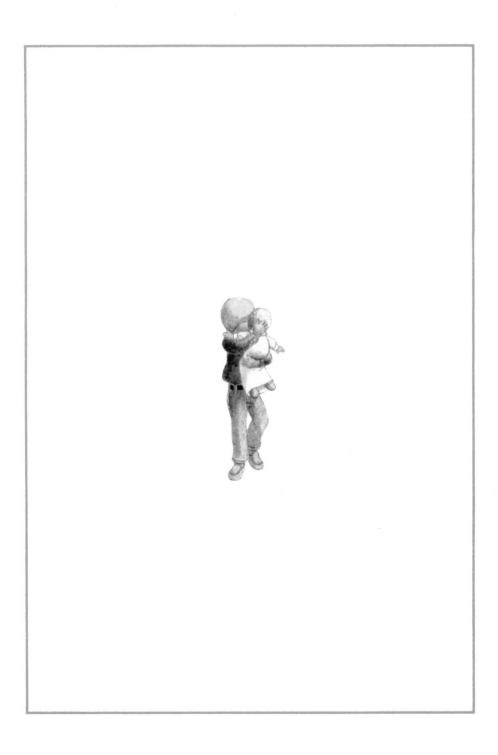

he'll know how to

take care of his baby

and feed him

and love him

and bring him

the things he wants,

like a doll

so that he can

practice being

a father."